MARKER

By Anna Kang   Illustrated by Christopher Weyant

Published by Two Lions, New York · www.apub.com · Amazon, the Amazon logo,

and Two Lions are trademarks of Amazon.com, Inc., or its affiliates.

ISBN-13 (hardcover): 9781542039611 · ISBN-13 (ebook): 9781542039598

The illustrations are rendered in ink and watercolor with brush pens

on Arches paper. · Book design by Abby Dening

Printed in China · First Edition

10 9 8 7 6 5 4 3 2 1

For the teachers and mentors who were signposts in our lives.
Thank you, Judy Post, MaryAnn Christie, Rosemary Walsh, Teruko Craig,
Charles Shiro Inouye, Robert Estrin, Mark Jonathan Harris, Howard A. Rodman,
John Ridley, Mrs. Allen, and David M. Williams. —A. K. and C. W.

Good morning, Teacher Supplies!
I'd like to introduce our newest
TS team member, Pinking Shears.

My friends call me Pink.

But I'm not allowed to make mistakes.
Everything I do is permanent.
There are no second chances for *me*.

Oh no, blot that out too!

Ugh! It looks awful.
I can't do it!

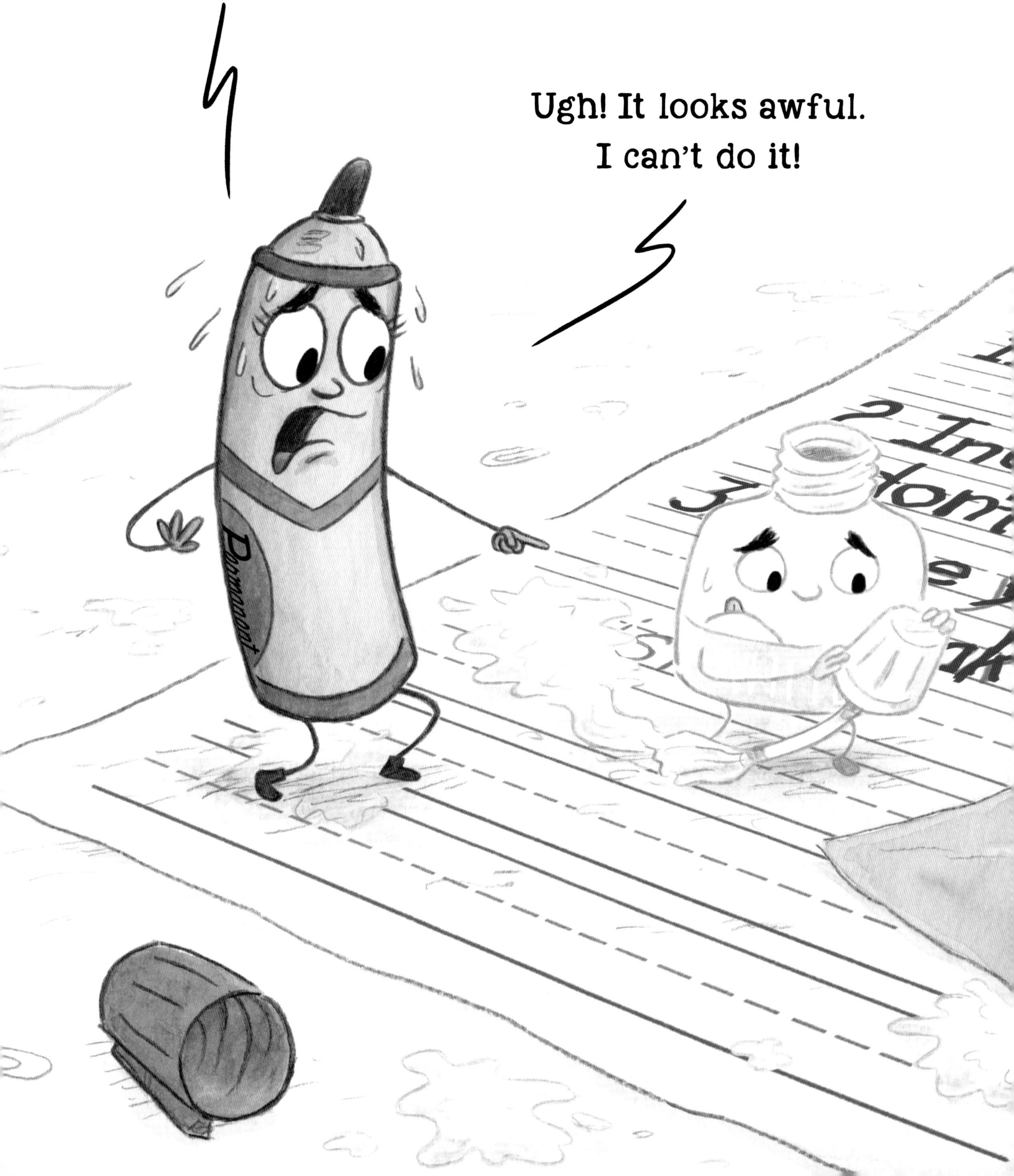

THE NEXT DAY...

Failure Fun Day!

During Free Choice today, everyone is going to try something new.

Something that seems difficult or just beyond your reach. We are going to have fun, get messy, and make mistakes.

Have fun . . .

get messy . . .

and make mistakes.

Thanks for believing in me.

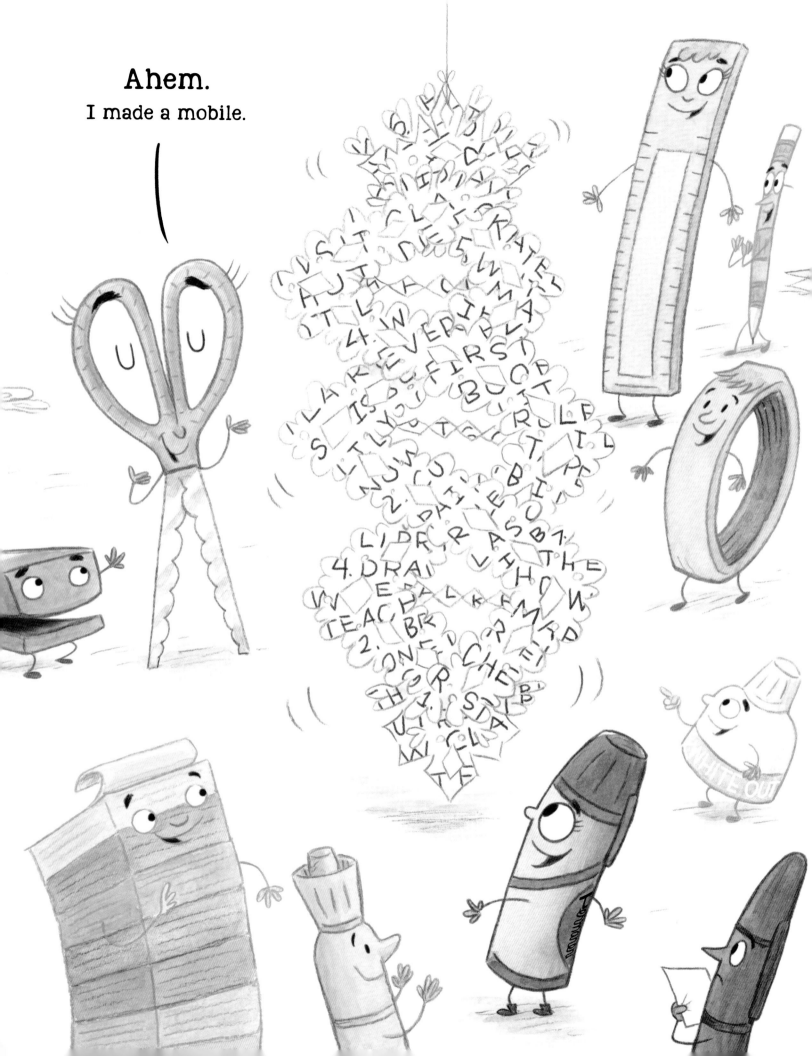